Hi there,

I'm David Warner, Australian cricketer,
and I'm really excited to introduce you to
my new series of kids' books called
The Kaboom Kid.

Little Davey Warner is 'the Kaboom Kid',
a cricket-mad eleven-year-old who wants to
play cricket with his mates every minute of
the day, just like I did as a kid.

Davey gets into all sorts of scrapes with his
friends, but mainly he has a great time playing
cricket for his cricket club, the Sandhill Sluggers,
and helping them win lots of matches.

If you're into cricket, and I know you are, then you
will love these books. Enjoy *The Kaboom Kid.*

David Warner

Hit For Six

DAVID WARNER

with J.S. BLACK, Illustrated by JULES FABER

SIMON & SCHUSTER
AUSTRALIA
A CBS COMPANY

THE KABOOM KID – HIT FOR SIX
First published in Australia in 2015 by
Simon & Schuster (Australia) Pty Limited
Suite 19A, Level 1, 450 Miller Street, Cammeray, NSW 2062

10 9 8 7 6 5 4 3 2 1

A CBS Company
Sydney New York London Toronto New Delhi
Visit our website at www.simonandschuster.com.au

National Library of Australia Cataloguing-in-Publication entry
Creator: Warner, David Andrew, author.
Title: Kaboom Kid #4: Hit For Six/David Warner and J.S. Black.
ISBN: 9781925030846 (paperback)
                  9781925030853 (ebook)
Target Audience: For children.
Subjects: Warner, David Andrew.
                  Cricket – Australia – Juvenile literature.
                  Cricket players – Australia – Juvenile literature.
                  Cricket – Batting – Juvenile literature.
                  Other Creators/Contributors: Black, J. S., author.
Dewey Number: 796.3580994

Cover and internal design by Hannah Janzen
Cover and internal illustrations by Jules Faber
Inside cover photograph of adult David Warner by © Quinn Rooney/Getty Images
Typeset by Midland Typesetters, Australia
Printed and bound in India by Replika Press Pvt. Ltd.

DEDICATED TO
THE MEMORY OF
PHILLIP HUGHES

CONTENTS

CHAPTER 1
THE BET

'Come on, show me what you've got!' Davey Warner teased George Pepi, tapping his bat impatiently at the crease.

George pounded down the rough run-up at Flatter Park and let fly his fastest delivery.

Davey watched the ball leave George's hand and danced down the pitch to meet it. He swung hard into the ball and . . .

Kaboom!

Davey smacked the ball high into the mid-wicket outfield. He watched with glee as his dog Max let out a yelp in protest. The fox terrier had been fielding at silly mid-off and was surprised at the direction Davey had hit the ball.

'Fooled you, Max!'

It wasn't easy to get one over on Max, who took off at full pelt after the ball. The foxy loved cricket just as much as Davey and his mates.

This was lucky, because playing cricket was all they ever wanted to do. The boys

often enjoyed having a hit at Flatter Park on Sundays. It was close to Davey, George and Sunil's homes and Benny's shop was opposite, which was handy for snack breaks.

Max clamped his sharp teeth down on the leather while performing a perfect mid-air 180-degree spin.

'I've had enough of bowling!' George complained, flexing his hand. Davey had been hitting him all over Flatter Park and his hand was getting cramped.

'Music to my ears,' said Sunil Deep, who went to the bowler's end. He much preferred bowling to keeping wicket.

Davey tapped his bat at the crease and waited. He wanted to practise hitting against Sunil's fast bowling. Davey had been feeling really good about his batting lately.

He'd been working really hard with his special bat Kaboom and it felt as if he'd just stepped up to a new level.

With a triumphant air, Max trotted back to Sunil and deposited the gooey ball at his feet. He whined expectantly.

'You're a machine, Max,' chuckled Sunil and gave the dog a scratch behind the ears.

'Here comes trouble,' murmured George.

Chief pest Mo Clouter and his equally annoying sidekicks, Nero and Tony, were walking out to the wicket.

'Just ignore them and they might go away.' Davey was impatient to play. 'Come on, Deep.'

'Why's Clouter dragging a suitcase around with him?' Sunil wondered aloud.

'Maybe he's moving away?' Davey suggested. They could always hope.

Max jumped up and ran towards Mo and sniffed at the suitcase eagerly.

'Has to be food,' said Davey. 'Max! Get back here!'

'I'm starving.' George clutched at his stomach.

'You're always starving,' Davey pointed out.

'Are you our new tea lady?' Sunil asked Mo.

Mo set the suitcase down at the end of the pitch. 'Laugh at me and you'll be sorry!'

'Why's that?' Davey gave up hope of having a hit anytime soon.

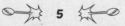

Mo gestured proudly to the suitcase. 'Because I have in my possession Benny's shop's entire stock of . . .' Mo unzipped the lid of the case to reveal . . .

'Whopper Chomps!' exclaimed George and Davey in unison.

The suitcase was indeed chock-a-block with packets of the chewy vampire teeth lolly that Davey and Sunil loved.

'You didn't steal them, did you?' asked Sunil suspiciously.

'I used up all my birthday money to buy them!' Mo stared lovingly at the brightly coloured lollies.

'What are you waiting for?' Davey said impatiently. 'Sharing is caring.'

Mo shook his head and crossed his arms on his chest.

'This is a new business venture. You're welcome to some of my stock, but it'll cost you.'

George narrowed his eyes at the unwelcome news. 'How much?'

'$3.50 a bag!' declared Mo.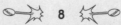

'Get out of town!' Davey was disgusted. 'You're charging fifty cents more than Benny does!'

'I'm not a charity!' Mo shrugged and explained his scheme. 'A man has to earn a living. It's called supply and demand. Benny won't have more stock for weeks, so in the meantime I'm the only supplier in the market.'

Davey rolled his eyes.

George checked his pockets for loose change. 'How much have you got, Davey? I've got $2.00.'

Davey grimaced. 'I'm broke. What about mate's rates?' he asked Mo.

Mo zipped up his case with a flourish. 'Last time I checked, we weren't mates.'

The bully had a point.

'There's a group of kids playing down by the swings. They could be *real* customers. Time is money . . .'

Mo turned to go.

'Hang on a minute,' said Davey. 'You can't get away with this!'

'I think he just did,' muttered George. His stomach let out a loud growl.

'It's nothing personal, Shorty. No, hang on, it *is* personal.' Mo cracked up laughing before heading off towards the playground, dragging his case behind him. He turned back and grinned. 'These are all mine . . . unless you're interested in having a bet.'

'I'm all ears,' said Davey.

'You've got the game against Shimmer Bay coming up in two weeks . . .'

'Yeah? So what?'

'If you hit six sixes, then I'll give you *all* my Whopper Chomps.'

'Six sixes?' George exclaimed. 'That's . . . like . . . impossible!'

'And if I don't hit six sixes?' Davey asked.

'You have to call me "My Lord and Master" for the rest for the season. You have to carry my footy kit, do my chores. Basically, you'll be my slave.'

'Don't do it, Davey,' Sunil warned.

Davey ignored Sunil. His eyes were fixed on Mo. He'd had enough of the big chump.

'It's a deal.' The words were out of Davey's mouth before he realised he'd said them.

'We each have witnesses, right?'

The others nodded.

Mo held out one of his enormous paws to shake Davey's hand.

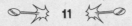

'It's a bet!' said Davey as he firmly gripped Mo's hand.

'See you, suckers!' Mo laughed slightly hysterically before taking off with his suitcase.

'You must *really* like Whopper Chomps!' George shook his head at Davey in disbelief.

Davey was up for the challenge. He was looking forward to spending every waking minute of the next two weeks practising his batting so he could bring Mo Clouter down a peg or two. It was way overdue.

CHAPTER 2

MASCOT MADNESS

Monday mornings at Sandhill Primary began with school assembly out in the quadrangle. Davey was usually late and this morning was no exception.

'Ssh!' Davey held a finger to his lips and slunk in to a place next to his friend

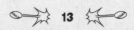

Kevin McNab. He was hoping his teacher
Mr Mudge wouldn't notice. Mudge hated
students being late. He hated it almost as
much as he hated cricket.

'What's this I hear about a bet?' Kevin asked.

Mudge's radar was in fine form. His head
spun around at lightning speed at the sound of
Kevin's voice. His ears glowed menacingly like
hot coals on an open fire.

'No talking!' Mudge hissed at Kevin. He
shot Davey a frown for good measure, before
turning back to gaze with a look of reverence
at their principal, Mrs Trundle.

Trundle had a lot to say, as always. She
rattled on about cake stalls, fundraisers, and
the upcoming art show and then – just when
it seemed she was wrapping things up – she
announced a list of merit award winners.

 14

Davey switched off. His name wouldn't be called out. It would be the same students who always won merit awards. Sunil and Bella Ferosi would be among them.

'Sunil Deep,' Mrs Trundle said brightly as she scanned the crowd for Sunil. He stood up and gave her one of his most winning dimpled smiles.

'If I hit six sixes, maybe I'll win a merit award,' Davey whispered to Kevin.

The crowd clapped wearily as Sunil accepted his piece of paper.

'Anything's possible,' Kevin whispered back.

'P-lease,' hissed a voice from behind Davey. Davey didn't need to turn around to know who the voice belonged to. Bella Ferosi.

She knew a lot about winning merit awards and was easily the best student in the class.

'You need *A*s, not *D*s, to win a merit award.' Bella always spoke slowly when speaking to Davey, as if she were speaking to a toddler. It was more than a little annoying.

'You know what, Bella?' whispered Davey.

Bella leaned in closer to hear what he had to say.

'I bet you that I win a merit award by the end of term.'

Kevin's eyes grew wide.

Bella waited for the punchline, but it didn't come. 'Oh, you're not joking?' She narrowed her eyes at Davey. 'That's a bet you're sure to lose.'

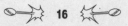

'Then you have nothing to lose by accepting the bet,' Davey smiled.

'And if by some freak chance you do win an award?' Bella asked.

'Then you have to dress up as the Sandhill Sluggers' mascot for our final game.'

A small worry line formed on Bella's perfect brow.

'Not the . . . *slug*?' Bella could hardly bring herself to say the word.

Nobody in their right minds ever wanted to wear the Sluggers' mascot costume. And for very good reason.

It was a dark grey–green slug colour with two brown slug antennae sticking dismally out the top. The slug dance was

like the moon walk – no arms, just legs
shuffling, dragging the slug's tail.

To make things worse, your face could be
seen while wearing the costume. There was
nowhere to hide.

'You're serious?' Bella seemed to warm to
Davey's idea thinking, perhaps, that there was
no way she could lose, because Mr Mudge
would *never* give Davey an award.

'And if – make that *when* – you don't win
an award, you'll join the All Stars cheer
squad for our netball final,' Bella said with
an evil grin.

'You mean, in a girl's netball uniform?'
Davey asked.

'Uh huh,' Bella nodded, 'pink skirt, pink
singlet, pink socks and pink shoes, and you

have to cheer the girls with the pompoms doing *all* the cheers.'

The cheers were ridiculous pop songs sung in soprano with lots of shrieking, giggling and girly hysteria. Something in Davey just snapped. If he was going to bring Mo down, he might as well do the same with Bella. Her opinion of herself was way too high.

'This is not a good idea, Davey,' Kevin warned.

'It's a bet,' said Davey and he shook Bella's outstretched hand.

She smiled politely before withdrawing her hand and wiping the palm on her tunic.

About a century later, assembly ended and they made their way to the classroom.

Mudge called for everyone to settle.

'Just a reminder that tomorrow is our exciting PE excursion to Penguin Palace RSL and Bowling Club and I expect you to be on your best behaviour,' their teacher explained, with something close to enthusiasm.

Mudge even looked less exhausted than usual as he spoke at length about his favourite sport, lawn bowls.

'It will be a long day out in the sun and it's a physically demanding sport . . .'

Davey caught George's eye. Mudge didn't know the meaning of physically demanding and rolling a ball down a small flat green certainly didn't cut it.

 20

'You'll need sunscreen, a hat, sports kit and don't be late for the bus. We leave at 8 a.m. sharp.' The bright vermilion of Mudge's ears highlighted the importance of his words.

Despite the fact that they were in for the world's most boring class excursion, Davey was looking forward to a day out of the classroom.

Surely it couldn't be all that bad?

Bella Ferosi's hand shot up.

'Yes, Bella?' Mudge asked, pleased that someone was showing an interest.

'Sir, will this excursion be assessed?' She shot Davey a smug look.

Mudge grinned. 'I'm so glad you asked, because that was my next announcement.'

Davey's stomach sank with a lurch. It landed somewhere around his knees.

Mudge was grinning from ear to ear like a deranged Cheshire cat. 'Your big assignment for the end of term will be an essay on lawn bowls.'

Davey groaned.

'*Warner,*' Mudge erupted. He went from cold to hot so quickly that the veins in his ears throbbed dangerously. 'You had better be well behaved tomorrow or there will be con-se-quences!'

Davey heard a snigger from Mo.

'Now, as preparation for tomorrow, we will spend the rest of the day studying the history of lawn bowls. If you'll turn your attention to . . .'

And the rest of the day proved to be as mind-numbing as Davey had thought it would be.

CHAPTER 3

ALARM BELLS

The end-of-day school bell rang out loud and clear.

'The bus leaves at 8 a.m. SHARP!' Mudge yelled as 6M shot out of the classroom as if their lives depended on it.

'I thought he'd never stop,' groaned Kevin.

Davey's head was so full of lawn bowls facts *he* felt old and crotchety.

'I can't believe you've bet your brains and your brawn,' joked George when they were getting their bikes from the bike racks near the school entrance.

'Bella could do with a little healthy competition,' Davey said.

Sunil stifled a laugh.

Davey shot his friend a look which said *Don't you start.* 'I can get a merit award if I set my mind to it.'

'And pigs can fly!' Sunil cracked up.

'Watch it,' Davey said.

'Ooh!' Sunil pretended to be scared. 'Let's see you put that attitude into your batting practice, because you're going to need it!'

'Race you to Little Park,' yelled Davey, taking off in front of the others on his pushie.

'Not if I get there first!' Kevin took off after Davey.

When they got to Little Park, the friends ditched their bikes and got down to business. Davey batted, Sunil bowled, Kevin took his place as wicket-keeper and George was fielder.

While Mudge had been droning on, Davey had spent the day planning his training regime for the next two weeks. He needed to practise his strokeplay, especially hooking, pulling and driving; *then* he wanted to hit sixes.

'Sunil, bowl me some long hops,' Davey asked.

Sunil slyly pitched the ball right up in the blockhole and Davey struggled to get the ball away at all, never mind hitting it for a six.

'Come on! None of this defensive stuff . . . I want to go big!'

Sunil got down to bowling him some long hops and Davey practised his big hits. He focused on following through with his shots. The ball repeatedly soared out of the park.

Sunil nodded at him. 'Better, though the bowlers you'll be facing are faster than me. You're going to need a few magic tricks.'

Davey soon realised what Sunil meant. His arms and shoulders quickly grew tired after slogging the ball over and over again.

Finally he had to admit defeat and call it a night. His shoulders were aching like nothing else.

After dinner, Davey brushed his teeth but even the effort of moving the brush up and down was agony.

'You need to toughen up,' he told the mirror.

Davey flexed his biceps and checked out his reflection. He grimaced at his sore muscles.

Davey's older brother, Steve, appeared in the doorway.

'Hey, Rambo,' Steve teased.

Davey grunted and continued brushing.

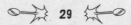

'I heard something about a bet with Mo. You reckon you're going to hit six sixes at the game against Josh Jarrett?' Steve asked.

Josh Jarrett was Shimmer Bay's captain and cricket's all-round Mr Perfect. Josh and Davey enjoyed a long-running grudge match.

As far as Davey was concerned, losing to Josh was something he couldn't bear to think about.

'Mmm.' Davey rinsed his mouth with mouthwash.

'I'll be there to cheer you on,' said Steve, clapping Davey on the back.

Whoosh! Davey spat out the mouthwash.

'You think I have a shot at winning?' He was stunned to think his brother had faith in him.

'Mate, you've got Buckley's.' Steve chuckled and grabbed his own toothbrush.

Davey groaned. He didn't have the energy to argue. He dragged himself down the hall and flopped into bed.

As soon as Davey opened his eyes, he knew something was wrong. The room was too bright, the house too quiet. He rolled over in bed and looked at his digital clock.

8 a.m.!!!

The digits flashed at him urgently. Davey's brain was sparked into life with a jolt. He'd been so tired the night before he'd forgotten to set his alarm.

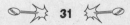

'AAAHHH!' Davey sat upright. He felt real and immediate terror. The bus for their excursion was leaving at 8 a.m.!

Mudge would be mad as a maggot.

Max bounded into the room and jumped onto Davey's bed. He looked happy and carefree.

'Move, dog!'

Davey pushed Max out of the way and leapt out of bed. If he hurried, he might still make it!

CHAPTER 4
THE HITCHHIKER

Davey sprinted down Eel Avenue towards
school. His backpack bumped jerkily,
digging into his spine. Despite his stiff
shoulder muscles, he pumped his arms like
pistons to sprint as fast as he could.

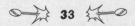

'You can do this,' he told himself between gasps for breath.

Just as Davey reached the corner of the street and could see the school grounds, he heard the familiar sound of claws on cement running alongside him.

'Max,' he hissed, 'go home now!'

Max refused to do anything of the sort. Davey lunged at the dog. The foxie bounded past Davey's outstretched arms and raced across the road towards school.

'Ugh! You mongrel!' Davey yelled.

He sprinted around the corner just in time to see a large bus pull out from the kerb.

'No! Wait!'

Davey sprinted as fast as he could after the bus but it accelerated as it pulled into the traffic. He felt as if his lungs might explode and reluctantly slowed to a halt. He bent over to catch his breath. Max jumped up and licked his face.

'I have two words for you,' muttered Davey, pushing the pesky dog away. 'Dog pound.'

For once Max looked contrite. He sat down abruptly and smiled with a butter-wouldn't-melt expression on his face.

'You don't fool me, mutt.' Davey tried not to panic and thought about his options. There was nothing to be gained by going to school now. He'd end up doing chores for Mrs Trundle all day.

In fact, the more Davey thought about it the better he felt. Suddenly he had an entire day free to practise hitting sixes!

'You're brilliant, Max!'

Max wagged his tail. He'd apparently known this all along.

'Warrr-*ner*!' A familiar drawl interrupted Davey's dreams of the perfect way to spend a day.

'Eh?' Davey turned to see Mr Mudge staring at him from the other side of the street.

'Why aren't you on the bus?' asked Mudge, whose ears were beginning to turn a magnificent magenta.

'I'm sorry, Sir, I slept in and missed it,' called Davey. He glared down at Max. *This is all your fault.*

'Lucky for you I'm taking my own car, so I can give you a lift!' Mudge replied cheerily.

Davey had never seen his teacher look so . . . *happy.* He noticed Mudge's old pale blue Morris Minor parked outside the front of the school. The teacher unlocked the car and opened the front passenger door.

'Hop in. I'll just grab some paperwork from the office and we can go.'

Davey exhaled a long sigh. He couldn't play cricket, but at least he wouldn't get into trouble with his mum or Mudge.

The only problem was he needed to get rid of Max before Mudge saw him. Mudge hated Max. The dog was banned from school grounds, but that had never stopped him – a fact which caused Mudge much displeasure.

'Go home, Max!' Davey commanded and pointed in the direction of Eel Avenue. He didn't have time to take the dog there.

Max cocked his head and ignored Davey completely. Then, quick as a flash, Max leapt into Mudge's car and curled up on the passenger seat.

'No way, Max!'

Davey had just about had enough of the dog's hijinks. 'Mudge hates you even more than he hates me, and that's a lot.'

Max seemed unmoved by Davey's revelation.

Then Davey caught a glimpse of Mudge's mustard-coloured skivvy and panicked.

'Quick, Max!' He unzipped his backpack and beckoned for the pesky pooch to get inside it. Max loved curling up in small spaces, so he trotted into the backpack and settled into a tight ball with his head sticking out of the opening.

'Keep quiet, or else!' Davey warned him. 'Just remember – dog pound.'

'Seat belt on please, Warner.' Mudge took his seat and started the engine.

Davey hugged his backpack to his chest so that Max's face was hidden. It wriggled slightly.

'Come on, boy. Throw your bag in the back, there's plenty of room,' Mudge commanded.

'Ah, no, it's fine here, thanks.' Davey gingerly placed the backpack at his feet and buckled his seat belt.

Within moments, the sound of Max's gentle snores drifted up from the floor.

Davey coughed loudly. 'Do you have any music, Sir?' he asked.

'As a matter of fact, the wireless is tuned to Classic FM,' Mudge smiled at Davey. He reached over and soon the car was flooded with the sound of classical music.

Davey thought it sounded like cats fighting, but at least it drowned out Max's snoring.

The drive to Penguin Palace Bowling Club would only take about ten minutes in a normal car with a normal driver. Mudge,

however, took slow driving to a new level.
He never allowed the speedometer to go above
40 kilometres an hour.

It was going to be a very long trip.

CHAPTER 5

THE CURVE BALL

Mudge parked in front of the Penguin Palace
Bowling Club.

'Hurry up and get carrying, Warner,'
Mudge instructed. 'I have some of my
own bowling ball collection that needs to
come inside.' He opened the boot of the

car to reveal boxes upon boxes of lawn
bowls.

'All of these,' Mudge clicked his fingers
at Warner. 'Be careful, they're heavy,'
he added before disappearing inside
the club.

Davey was on his third trip carrying boxes
when the bus finally pulled up.

'Oi, Teacher's Pet!' Mo squashed his huge
gob against the bus window and made faces
at Davey.

Bella Ferosi jumped up to see who Mo was
talking to. Teacher's Pet was *her* nickname!
She seemed perturbed to see Davey working
as Mudge's personal helper.

'Getting a merit award by sucking up
to the teacher doesn't count!' she whispered

threateningly to Davey as she sashayed
past and grabbed a box of lawn bowls
to carry.

Once everyone was off the bus and inside
the club, Mudge called for quiet.

'This is my club. You had all better be
squeaky clean and your best selves today or
you will live to regret it. Am I clear?'

'Crystal, Sir,' the class droned in unison.

'Hear that, Max?' Davey whispered to his
bag. The bag huffed.

Mudge divided the class into four groups.
Davey and George were on the same team,
Sunil and Kevin in another. Mo and Bella
were in another still.

Sunil picked up a bowling ball from the box. 'Weird shape,' he commented. 'Just like your head, Mo!'

George cracked up. Mo glared at him and grabbed a bowl from the box. He drew back his arm and sent it hurtling dangerously down the green. The ball veered sharply to the right and careered off into the gutter.

'Oi, my ball is broken!' Mo shouted.

'Keep your voice down, Mr Clouter! There are other people trying to play here.' Mudge smiled apologetically at the other members playing on a rink further down the green.

'As Mr Clouter here has just shown us,' Mudge explained to the group through clenched teeth, 'the bowls are not round.'

He held up a bowl to demonstrate.

'That's just dumb,' Mo huffed.

'The aim of the game is to get your black bowling ball as close to the white jack as possible,' continued Mudge.

'Now, this isn't as easy as it looks. It takes precision, skill and lots of practice.'

Davey shot Sunil a look. *Come on . . . !* Mudge was talking about a tiny square piece of lawn made up of perfectly manicured grass. It was nothing like a cricket pitch and certainly didn't require any muscle.

As Mudge explained more about the game, he looked as close to contented as Davey had ever seen him.

'The bowls are weighted to one side so they will curve towards the place you want to hit. How much it turns depends on how fast you roll it and where you aim it. Rather than straight, you are aiming to send the bowl in an arc shape.'

Mudge selected a bowl and held it out to Bella. 'Miss Ferosi, why don't you have a try?'

With a firm flick of her ponytail, Bella accepted the challenge. She rolled her bowl down the green in a perfect arc and it came to a rest just beside the target.

Mudge's pale face flushed with pleasure and he burst into a spontaneous round of applause. 'Someone in this class was paying attention! Thank you, Bella!'

Bella shot Davey a 'beat that' look.

A flash of colour and movement caught Davey's eye.

'Uh oh,' he sucked in his breath.

Davey's backpack was heading inside the club towards the bar. He'd forgotten all about Max! While Mudge droned on, Davey excused himself, saying he needed to go to the toilet.

'Max!' Davey hastily grabbed the backpack and carried it with him to the toilets. He unzipped the bag and gave the dog a drink of water.

'You need to lie low for a little while longer,' he told the dog.

Max bristled.

'Come on,' coaxed Davey.

Max gave a low growl.

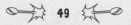

'I'll make it worth your while, I promise,' Davey pleaded. 'Lots of doggie treats!'

Finally Max stalked slowly into the backpack and lay down with a huff. Davey placed the backpack carefully alongside the other bags. When he joined the group again, Mudge was demonstrating how to bowl using the shape of the ball to its best advantage. 6M clapped on cue as he sent a ball rolling at a snail's pace down the green.

Then Mudge announced he would give each student an individual lesson. It would take about two thousand years to get through them all.

'Wake me up when it's my turn,' whispered Kevin. He closed his eyes and rested his head against a pole.

'Warner!' Mudge barked.

Davey jumped to attention. 'Yes, Sir!'

'Let's see what the mighty cricketer can do!' Mudge licked his lips.

Davey selected a bowl and felt its weight. He judged the distance to the jack and tried to picture the arc the ball would travel along. He drew a line in his mind's eye.

As the bowl left Davey's hand, he saw a white blur flash through the corner of his eye.

No!

Max was tearing across the green after the ball.

'Max!'

It was all too horrible. Max ignored Davey's
ball and plucked the jack from the green and
held it expertly between his teeth.

'WARNER!' Mudge roared. 'Get that
dog off the green!' He sounded close to
hysterical and his ears had turned a bright
fire-engine red.

Mo's laugh broke out through the chaos
and Davey turned to see the bully lying on
the ground in stitches. He writhed around,
pointing and laughing.

Max had gone crazy – now that he was
free he was tearing around in circles, barking
in a frenzy. But the real problem was that,
every time he changed direction, he tore up
big tufts of green turf which flew into the air
like confetti.

CHAPTER 6

MAD MAX

Max was like a dog possessed as he zigged and zagged across the square green.

A crowd had gathered from inside the club room. Horrified *oohs* and *ahs* soon drowned out Mo's maniacal laughter.

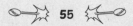

'Max, you monster!' Davey tried to grab Max, but the foxie was having none of it. He dodged and weaved like a football pro. At one point he stopped and, for a second, Davey thought he had a chance to grab him.

But the dog began to furiously dig a hole in the green. Then he dropped the small white ball neatly into it.

'Max!'

Then, to top it off, Max cocked his back leg and peed into the hole.

It brought everyone to a standstill. There was a horrified silence which was broken by the sound of Mo laughing again.

Davey buried his head in his hands.

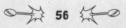

The crowd burst into stunned but slightly admiring applause at the audacity of the small dog.

'WARNER!' Mudge erupted. He was positively apoplectic. His ears were almost black. 'Get that dog off the green NOW!'

Sunil, Kevin, George and Davey closed in on Max. The mad mutt lay down and rolled over, completely tuckered out. Sunil picked him up and tucked him firmly under one arm. He gave Davey a look of sympathy.

Max had done a lot of damage in a very short amount of time. Now the green was less a green colour and more a brown patchwork pattern. Aside from the clumps of dirt, Max had dug two decent-sized holes.

Mudge walked around the green muttering to himself. Then he went unusually quiet.

The excursion was cancelled.

Davey was doomed.

'There, there,' crooned Bella with delight, patting him on the back.

Mo was still laughing.

Back at school, Davey had to suffer through Mo and his cronies' endless sniggering, Bella's superior smiles and general loathing from the rest of the class. He was officially an outcast, as the whole of 6M blamed him for ruining a day out and having to be back at school before lunchtime.

'I want a word with you, Warner,' Mudge drawled as the bell finally rang for the end of day.

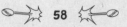

It was the first time the teacher had spoken to him since they left the bowls club.

Good luck, Sunil mouthed to Davey as he and the others filed out of class.

'As punishment for your dog's appalling behaviour today' – Mudge spoke so quietly that Davey strained to hear him – 'you will volunteer at the bowling club every day for the next two weeks.'

Davey opened his mouth to protest, but thought better of it. He would still have time to practise cricket before school.

'By every day, I mean before school and after school,' Mudge continued.

Davey whimpered. He thought about his two bets and how impossible it was going to be to win either.

'I have already spoken to your mother,' Mudge continued, looking at his desk. He was so angry he couldn't even look at Davey. 'Personally, I don't want you anywhere near my club, but it was their decision. You will start work tomorrow morning.'

'Mr Mudge . . .' Davey began.

'Are we understood?' Mudge brought his fist down hard on his desk with a thump.

Davey jumped.

'Yes, Sir!'

Davey left the classroom and made his way over to the nets for cricket practice. The team had already begun having a hit, but their coach Benny was nowhere to be seen.

'What's the punishment?' George asked.

'I've got to spend the next two weeks at the bowls club.'

Sunil's eyes grew round. 'Mate, you have no chance of winning the bet. Call it off with Mo now.'

'No!' Davey said stubbornly. 'I don't give up on a bet.'

'Suit yourself,' Sunil answered.

Just then, Benny arrived. 'Gather round, lads,' he called, trying to get his breath back.

The team gathered around their coach.

'Our next game is a bye and then we have the big one with Shimmer Bay.' Benny stuck a porky finger into one nostril and had a good dig.

'We have no chance. I just want you guys to do your best. It's all we can hope for.'

'Do you have a strategy, coach?' asked George.

Benny stared off into the distance. 'Not as such. Just watch out for that Josh Jarrett. He's a player to watch. Going places he is.'

Davey kicked at the dirt with his foot.

Benny glanced at his watch. 'Is that the time? Got to get home for tea.' He waddled off in the direction of his shop.

Sunil rolled his eyes at Benny's departure and the team went back to their cricket practice while it was still light enough to play.

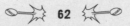

'What are you going to write for your lawn bowls assignment?' Practice was over and Sunil was packing up his kit.

'I thought I'd write about the bias,' said Kevin.

George shrugged. 'I liked the team spirit.'

'Warner?' Sunil asked.

Davey shook his head, 'Dunno, Deep. I really haven't given it much thought.'

'You should,' Sunil replied, 'if you want to beat Bella and win a merit award. It's our last major assessment for the term.'

'Thanks for the advice . . .' Davey muttered. He grabbed his Kaboom bat and marched off home.

Davey was about to spend all his spare time at a bowling club. The last thing he wanted to do was think about Mudge, or anything to do with lawn bowls, for that matter.

CHAPTER 7

AGAINST THE BIAS

Davey had made sure to set his alarm for an early start the next morning. It would take at least half an hour to ride to Penguin Palace Bowling Club and they wanted him to put in a full hour of work before school.

When he wheeled his bike inside the club gate, Davey shuddered at the sight that met his eyes. The green looked as if a herd of elephants had stampeded across it. He had a flashback to the sight of Max peeing in the hole. The horror!

'You must be David!' a tanned, grey-haired man wearing faded green overalls greeted him.

'Everyone calls me Davey,' Davey replied, 'except Mr Mudge, of course.'

The man straightened up from weeding the flowerbed and smiled. 'And what does Vernon, I mean Mr Mudge, call you?'

'WARRR-*NER*!' Davey replied, giving his best impersonation of Mudge.

The old man chuckled.

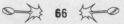

'Nice to meet you, Davey. I'm Trevor and I'm the greenkeeper here.'

They shook hands. Trevor glanced at Davey's backpack.

'Is there a dog in your bag, by any chance?'

'Uh, no,' Davey squirmed, 'not this time, anyway.'

'Made quite a mess, he did. Some of the members were very upset,' Trevor continued.

Davey shoved his hands in his pockets and stared at the ground. 'I – I – I'm really sorry,' he stuttered.

'Thanks Davey.' Trevor lowered his voice. 'This lot need stirring up every now and then, if you ask me.'

Davey looked up. He wasn't sure, but
he thought he saw a twinkle in the old
man's eye.

'Do you like lawn bowls?' Trevor asked.

'Yeah?' Davey sounded about as convincing
as Benny did when asked if the Sluggers had a
chance.

Trevor nodded. 'It's not for everyone. Grab
some gloves and get to work weeding with
me. I'm sure you're not too pleased to be here,
but I'm grateful for some help. My back's not
what it used to be.'

Davey thought Trevor looked really fit
and strong for his age. 'What about the green?'
he asked.

'We'll get to that. Plenty of time.'

Davey picked up a pair of gardening gloves and got to work. He hadn't even noticed the gardens when he was here for the excursion. The bowling green was surrounded by garden beds filled with flowers and small shrubs.

Weeding was boring, but after a while Davey kind of zoned out and didn't mind it so much. Trevor whistled as he worked and it was nice to be outside in the fresh air. It was better than being in detention or picking up rubbish at school.

'You'll probably want to get off to school soon,' Trevor said when they had finished the final garden bed.

Davey stretched. His shoulders and back ached. He'd never realised gardening was such physical work. 'See you this afternoon, then,' he said and picked up his bag.

He was wheeling his bike out when he noticed a familiar face.

It was Josh Jarrett. He was walking to school with a few other boys from Shimmer Bay Primary.

Davey thought about turning around, but it was too late. Josh had seen him.

'Warner?' Josh called. 'Given up on cricket, then?'

'You wish,' Davey retorted.

'Maybe it's time for you to retire. Lawn bowls might be more your speed!' Josh erupted in fits of laughter.

Trevor and Davey shared a look.

'I heard about your little bet!' Josh continued. 'Warner here reckons he can hit six sixes during our game,' he explained to his mates.

Everyone burst out laughing.

'That little squirt?' asked one of Josh's friends.

Josh nodded and pointed at Davey.

Davey said nothing. Trevor looked intrigued.

'Six sixes in a game against me . . . ?' Josh slapped his knee. 'You're dreaming!'

Davey met Josh's gaze coolly. He was becoming immune to others laughing at him. 'See you at the game, Josh.'

Josh walked off laughing.

'Let me guess: he's an excellent cricket player, even if he is a bit arrogant,' Trevor said.

'His team is current number one and he also plays for the rep side.'

'Yep, I hate him already.'

Trevor pulled his cap further down his head and got back to work. 'See you this arvo, then.'

Davey took that as a signal to head off to school.

He thought about what Josh had said as he rode to school. He now had very little time to practise big-hitting and Josh would make sure everyone found out about the bet.

Davey was going to be the laughing stock of the whole town.

CHAPTER 8
SLEEP ON IT

For the rest of the day, Davey couldn't stop yawning. This gave Mudge a great deal of satisfaction.

'Tired from doing some honest work for once, Warner?' the teacher asked with a smirk.

Davey thought he had a nerve – Mudge was always exhausted.

'That's the trouble with your generation – no work ethic.' This inspired Mudge to launch into a monologue about how the values of 'young people these days' were on the decline.

Davey blocked Mudge out. He was thinking about how to get some cricket training into his already packed week.

At least Mudge seemed to have calmed down about the Max incident now Davey was serving his penance.

Mo, on the other hand, wouldn't leave Davey alone. 'Not much time for batting practice with all the gardening you'll be doing!' he whispered to Davey while Mudge's back was turned.

'That was low,' Davey hissed back. 'How can I practise my hitting if I'm stuck at the bowls club every waking minute?'

Mo leaned in so close that Davey could smell his breath. *Phee-ew!*

'Not my problem, Warner.'

'Can I help you two?' Davey looked up to see Mudge standing over them both.

'No thank you, Sir,' said Mo innocently. 'David and I were just discussing the lawn bowls assignment, Sir.'

This placated Mudge, who went back to droning on about wayward youth and how unemployable they all were.

Mo winked at Davey. 'No Whopper Chomps for you, Warner.'

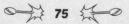

Davey didn't reply. As much as he hated to admit it, Mo had him. He had him right where he wanted him.

Sunil, Kevin and George were still playing cricket at Little Park when Davey rode his bike there that evening. He'd come straight from the bowls club. There were still a few minutes left of daylight and Davey had been itching to practise a new batting trick he'd thought about all day.

'Guys, the legendary MS Dhoni had a brilliant helicopter hit that always got him sixes,' he announced, picking up Sunil's bat to demonstrate. The famous Indian player would hit the ball upwards and then follow through with his bat twirling above his shoulders in a circular motion. When played well, it looked like a helicopter rotor.

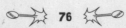

Sunil guffawed. 'This I've got to see.'

'I know, I need to practise it, but maybe
I could use it to hit a six off a good-length
ball.' Davey stifled a yawn. 'Borrow your bat?'
he asked Sunil.

'Sure, I'll bowl.'

Davey grabbed his helmet and fastened the
straps. This was a trick that required head
protection.

Sunil walked back up to his mark and
turned to face Davey. Kevin got into position
as wicket-keeper and George fielded at
first slip.

Sunil went easy on Davey and the first ball
was slow compared to what he'd have to face
against Shimmer Bay. He swung hard at the
ball and tried to spin around in a circular

movement after the bat. He spun so fast he nearly fell over.

'You need strong arms and a really fast bat speed for the helicopter shot to work,' Sunil pointed out.

Davey knew his mate was right.

'Bowl on a good length,' Davey instructed, 'and let me see what I can do.'

Sunil bowled the next one short of a length and as it passed Davey at waist height, he swung at the ball but only succeeded in sending it straight up into the air.

The following ball was well up, but Davey swung too late and only managed to pop the ball straight back to Sunil.

'Not as easy as it looks on YouTube. It's hard to time it right,' Davey lamented.

But he kept practising and after several more tries he succeeded in hitting a beauty right out of the park.

It was almost dark. 'Better go finish my essay for Mudge,' said Sunil.

'Don't tell me that's due tomorrow?' Davey asked with a groan.

'Okay, I won't!'

Davey gave him a look. 'Is it?'

Sunil nodded.

Davey sighed. He was utterly spent. 'Better get to it, then,' he muttered and headed across the road to his house.

Davey's mum had kept his dinner warm.
He realised he was starving and bolted down
his favourite meal of sausages and mash.

'Thanks, Mum!' Davey gave her a quick kiss
on the cheek and headed to his room.

He opened his schoolbook and stared
at the blank page. The lines began to blur.
His muscles were sore, his stomach was full.
It had been a long day.

Within minutes, his head had fallen onto
the desk. Davey was fast asleep.

CHAPTER 9

CAUGHT OUT

Davey spent the next morning before school helping Trevor at the bowling club. They laid new turf to try and patch the holes Max had made.

'Not bad,' said Trevor when he saw the job Davey had done. The green was already

beginning to look more green than brown. 'I'll water it while you're at school.

'*School*?' Davey checked his watch. He was going to be late!

Davey rode like crazy and made it to school just as class was about to begin. He slipped into the room and quietly took his seat. He felt a deep burn in his thighs from pedalling so fast. His muscles were going to stiffen up sitting all day.

Bella caught his eye and held up a piece of paper and mouthed the words 'A-plus' at him. Davey remembered with a jolt: *The essay!* He hadn't done it.

'Oh no!' Davey hoped like crazy that Mudge would forget to ask for their essays until after lunch. Maybe then he could write his during the lunch break.

'Shall I collect the essays?' Bella Ferosi asked Mudge, with a triumphant look at Davey.

Davey groaned. So much for that.

Mudge clapped his hands together eagerly. 'Thank you, Bella. Lovely to see someone with drive and initiative.'

Bella was out of her chair in less time than it took to say Teacher's Pet.

Davey shot Sunil a panicked look. The friends had to sit in opposite corners of the room so they couldn't talk about cricket. Mudge loathed cricket almost as much as he loathed students who didn't hand in their assignments.

Sunil understood immediately. He shot his hand up.

'Yes, Sunil?' Mudge asked.

Sunil flashed his dimple. 'I was wondering if you'd mind repeating yesterday's equations, Sir? I didn't quite understand.'

'Not like you, Mr Deep.' Mudge began writing out an equation on the whiteboard.

Davey gave Sunil the thumbs up. Maybe the distraction technique would work.

With his back still turned, Mudge asked Bella, 'Miss Ferosi, how are you going with those assignments?'

Or maybe not. Davey felt doomed.

Bella was making her way around the room slowly. She ticked each name off a list

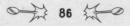

with a determined flourish as she collected
each paper.

'Nearly done, Mr Mudge.' Bella moved a
little faster.

'Take a seat, Miss Ferosi, I'll collect the
rest myself.'

Bella handed Mudge the pile of essays.
Mudge scanned the checklist.

'Just two to go. Mr Clouter and Mr Warner.'
Mudge held out his hand impatiently to Davey
and Mo.

Mo handed over two sheets of paper held
together by a silver paperclip. Mudge added it
to his pile.

'Warner?' Mudge clicked his fingers
impatiently. 'Come on, we don't have all day.'

Davey gulped. 'It's like this, Sir . . .'

Mudge raised an eyebrow. 'You're not going to tell us your dog ate your homework, are you, Warner?'

There were a few sniggers from around the room.

'Although, knowing your mutt, I wouldn't put it past him.'

Davey squirmed.

'With all the extra work at the bowling club, I . . .'

'*Yes?*' Mudge leaned over him.

'With all the extra work at the bowling club, I . . .'

'Spit it out, Warner!'

'I fell asleep, Sir,' Davey finished lamely.

Mudge rocked back and forth on his heels. 'A shining example to the rest of the class about the pitfalls of leaving everything to the last minute.'

'Sorry, Sir,' Davey added.

'You will be!' Mudge brightened up slightly. He obviously lived for moments like this. 'You're on lunchtime detention for the next two weeks. And I want that essay finished by Monday.'

'But with the work I'm doing at the bowling club, I won't have any time,' Davey argued.

'I *own* you for the next two weeks!' Mudge roared. '*Am I clear?!*'

Davey knew it was pointless to argue. 'Crystal, Sir.' He slumped lower in his seat.

Mo nudged him sharply with his elbow. 'Lord and Master,' he guffawed.

Bella, who sat on the other side of Davey, leaned in close to him. 'I hope you've been practising your cheers,' she smiled brightly.

Bella was right. In no time, Davey would be wearing a pink skirt and chanting netball songs. He was sunk.

Now Davey had absolutely no time to practise his big-hitting. And there was no way in the world he was going to win a merit award. He imagined wearing pink and cheering the netball team while Mo snacked on Whopper Chomps and Davey was his personal slave.

He couldn't bear to think about it.

CHAPTER 10

ROLLING, ROLLING, ROLLING

At the bowling club after school, Trevor led
Davey to the storage shed. Inside was a huge,
ancient-looking metal roller.

'You've got to be kidding.'

The roller looked more like a museum relic than a functioning piece of machinery.

'You know you can get ride-on rollers these days like they use on cricket pitches?' Davey asked.

'Is that so?' Trevor said with a wink. 'Well, we've got nothing that fancy here.'

He lifted the handle and began to pull. 'Stop your gawping and come and help me,' he said, straining against the weight. 'This thing weighs a ton.'

Davey grabbed the other side of the handle and helped Trevor pull the roller out onto the green. It was slow going. Like a slug.

'We've done the best we can with the grass. Just a matter of time before it grows back,'

Trevor explained. 'But now we need a level playing surface.'

'You want *me* to push this thing?' Davey asked.

Trevor looked around. 'I don't see anyone else lining up for the job, and I'll be mowing the professional green.'

He nodded his head for Davey to get to work.

Davey inspected the roller. *Yikes*.

'Okay. I can do this,' he told himself. He leaned down, picked up the steel handle and leaned all of his weight into it as he pushed. The roller barely moved.

Davey tried again. He grunted with the effort. The roller moved a few centimetres.

'Yes!'

There was a smattering of applause. 'That'll toughen you up,' said an old man who was watching him from the side of the green.

Another old codger gave Davey the thumbs up.

'Young people today don't know about physical work.'

The other oldie agreed and they fell into a whinge-fest about how things were so much harder back in their day.

'I'll show you wrinklies,' Davey muttered to himself. He braced his arms, keeping them slightly bent but strong, and leaned forward with all his might. The roller moved forward with a jolt and this time Davey was able to keep the momentum going.

After what felt like four hours but was only ten minutes, Davey had rolled three metres of green. He stopped for a break.

The old codgers were still watching and one of them motioned for him to join them.

'Not bad for a young punk,' said one.

'Thanks,' Davey said flatly. His shoulders were already beginning to ache.

'You know,' said the other codger, 'Trevor can roll this whole green in the time it took you to do that measly effort.'

Measly effort? That was a bit harsh.

'Has Trevor always worked here?' Davey asked.

'Old Trev? Nah, he used to work in cricket.'

Davey's ears pricked up. 'Cricket?'

'He looked after all the big pitches – The Gabba, SCG, you name it. The man knows his cricket. He has a few stories to tell, does Trev.'

The members fell back into their own conversation and Davey realised he'd been dismissed. If Trevor could do it, then Davey Warner could. He resolved to finish rolling the green.

He went back to the roller and gave it his all.

Davey was thoroughly exhausted by the time he got home. He'd had a major upper body workout at the bowls club, and a lower body workout on his pushie riding the ten kilometres there and back twice a day.

All he wanted to do was eat and go to bed as soon as he got home.

Davey's mum had other ideas. 'David Warner, get in here right now. You've got some explaining to do.'

Uh oh. Davey froze in the kitchen doorway, but he was too tired to make a run for it.

He found his mum pacing the lounge room. That was a bad sign.

She pointed to the couch. 'Sit.'

Davey sat down.

'I just don't understand,' his mum began. 'First there's this business with the bowls club and you and Max running riot. Now, Mr Mudge says you don't even bother handing in your assignments.'

Davey groaned. 'It wasn't like that, Mum.'

'If you put the same amount of effort into your schoolwork as you do into cricket, you'd be top of your class!'

'Sorry, Mum. I did try but I fell asleep.'

'Aha!' His mum pounced. 'Fell asleep because you're so tired from playing cricket every minute of the day. Well, that's all stopping right now.'

'Er, what's stopping?'

'Cricket. No more until you write the essay. I know you have a big game coming up, but you won't be playing in it until the work is done.'

'But Mum!' Davey wanted to explain about the bet and hitting six sixes, but he was worried it would make her even angrier.

He was starting to think she might be right.

His mum gave him some left-over corned beef and vegetables for dinner. He could barely lift the fork to his lips because he was so tired.

'Bed!' said his mum, once he'd eaten.

'Bed,' sighed Davey as he sank into his mattress.

He stretched out his aching shoulders and fell into a deep and dreamless sleep.

CHAPTER 11

BEHIND THE SCENES

Davey was finished.

He looked back over his work from the last few days and felt a deep sense of pride. His arm muscles felt it too. He had worked all weekend and the social players' bowling green was now perfectly rolled.

Trevor clapped him on the back. 'I think you deserve a break.'

Inside the club, Trevor bought Davey a club lunch and a lemonade. They sat together at a window table and looked out over the green.

'I heard a rumour that you used to look after cricket pitches,' said Davey before gulping down some lemonade.

Trevor chuckled. 'For most of my life.'

'Did you ever play?' Davey asked.

'As a kid I did, but later I liked watching more. I've seen lots of the big games. But I like the behind-the-scenes stuff better.'

The bartender brought their meals over and there was silence while they both tucked into hamburgers and chips. Davey realised he was ravenous.

'So how's Mr Mudge going, or should I call him Mudge?'

Davey rolled his eyes and finished chewing a mouthful of chips.

'He's on my case. I've got to hand in an essay tomorrow about lawn bowls and I don't know where to begin.'

'Why don't you write about what you've learned working here?'

'Gardening?'

'How to prepare a pitch for play. It's the same with cricket. As a player, you have to learn how to read the pitch. Someone has meticulously prepared that piece of grass

 **105**

to be level and the moisture of the soil has to be just right or cracks appear. What happens if a crack appears and you bowl or hit a ball onto it?'

Davey thought about the question. 'The ball could go in a direction different from where you expect it to.'

Trevor nodded. 'Exactly! So, in order to read a pitch or a bowling green properly, you need to learn how to maintain it. In bowls as in cricket, the condition of the grass affects the path and speed of the ball.'

Trevor had a point. Davey knew about the pitch affecting his game, but he'd always been rubbish at turning it to his advantage.

'If you can read a pitch correctly, then you might just be one step ahead of your mate Josh Jarrett.'

Davey realised for the first time that there might just *be* something to the game of lawn bowls.

'Want me to show you how to play bowls properly?'

Davey nodded.

Once they had finished their meal, Trevor collected a bag from the storage shed and took it with him out to the green. He unzipped it and pulled out two beautifully polished bowls. He handed one to Davey.

'You already know the bowl is shaped so that it will roll in a curved direction. Now, I know this green very well and I know that it's slightly uneven – it sinks a little lower in the left corner – so I'll keep that in mind when I play. Also, some greens are fast and some are slow. We have quite a slow green.'

They had a game and some of the members even gathered around to give tips. Davey realised that bowls was a very social sport and before too long he was enjoying himself.

'You can have a rest day tomorrow and then it's back to more rolling,' said Trevor, when it was time to head home.

'But it's all done,' protested Davey, pointing to the social green they'd been playing on.

'You're ready for the big league son,' Trevor chuckled, pointing to the professional players' green next to the one they had worked on.

Davey groaned.

That night, Davey tidied his room. He never tidied his room. Yet he found himself packing toys away, putting dirty clothes in the wash basket, and neatly lining up his cricket trophies so they faced out just so.

Once his room was spotless, he began to vacuum the lounge room floor.

Davey's mum eyed him suspiciously. 'As much as I love the fact that you're helping around the house,' she said, 'I think it's time to start your essay.'

'The dirty dishes are still in the sink!' protested Davey.

'Now!' His mother frogmarched him to his room and sat him down at his desk.

She was right. If he didn't hand his essay in the next day, he wouldn't be allowed to practise his hitting, let alone play in the match.

Max wandered into the room and jumped up onto Davey's bed.

'Hey, mutt,' said Davey.

Max circled three times and then lay down with a huff.

Davey yawned. He looked down at his blank piece of paper. Wow. He'd been sitting there for ten minutes and hadn't written a word.

Trouble is, maybe Bella's right, he thought. *Maybe I'm just not very academic. Mr Mudge doesn't seem to think I am.*

Davey really felt like a Whopper Chomp. Or something sugary to eat. Or anything to eat. Or a drink. He got up to go to the kitchen.

'Not so fast!' Davey's mum was waiting in the hall outside his bedroom.

'Are you stalking me?' Davey asked.

'Essay,' she said firmly.

'I'm hungry,' Davey complained.

Davey's mum smiled knowingly. 'I'll bring you a snack. And a drink. Now go!'

Davey sat back down at his desk and knew that this was it. No more excuses. He thought about Trevor and the care and attention that went into looking after the bowling green.

Davey wrote at the top of the page, 'Behind the Scenes by David Warner'.

Then he began to write.

CHAPTER 12

BAD GUYS AND UNDERDOGS

The next morning, Davey met up with Sunil, Kevin and George at C playing field before school.

'Hey, stranger,' called Kevin. Then he hit a ball straight into George's outstretched hands at silly mid-off.

'Howzat?' cried George.

'Aw!' Kevin walked.

Davey and Kaboom took their place at the crease. It felt good to be back. Sunil obliged by bowling him a few so he could practise his new shot.

'Woah!' Davey realised just how rusty he was when he spun around so fast he fell over.

'You'll be calling me Lord and Master before too long,' snorted Mo, who seemed to have appeared magically out of thin air.

Mo was flanked by Nero and Tony, who apparently both found Mo's comment to be utterly hilarious.

Davey knew it was better to ignore Mo in the hope he would vanish, but this morning he took the bait.

'You don't know what you're talking about, Clouter,' he said. 'You know nothing about cricket.'

'I know you've done zero cricket practise for the last week,' the big galah screeched. 'The Whopper Chomps are mine, *all mine!*'

'Don't be too sure,' said Davey. 'I'm the underdog and everyone loves the underdog.'

'The chances of you hitting six sixes are zero,' the big hunk of wood guffawed before lumbering off.

Davey managed to get a few hits in before the bell rang.

The four friends made their way to the classroom. Most of 6M had already taken their seats, but Mudge was nowhere to be seen.

Bella Ferosi gave her ponytail a distracted flick when she saw Davey take his seat.

'End of term is getting closer, David,' she said and held up her pocketbook calendar. 'Not much time left to get a merit award.'

Bella flashed Davey her perfectly even white teeth in a well-practised, yet insincere, smile.

'So should I measure you up for a costume?' she continued. 'Pink will really suit your skin tone.'

'Just like slug colour will really suit yours,' Davey shot back.

They locked eyes.

Davey waggled two fingers above his head like slug antennae waving in the breeze.

'Don't mess with me, Warner,' Bella replied, her voice as cold as steel. 'There's only room in this class for one teacher's pet.'

Davey mimed the slug dance and hummed the Sluggers' song.

Finally Mr Mudge arrived.

'Good morning, 6M.' He dabbed at the back of his neck with a stained handkerchief. 'We have computer studies first up this morning, so grab your workbooks and we'll head over to the lab.'

Davey shot up his hand.

'What is it, Warner?' Mudge snapped, with more than a hint of impatience.

'I have my lawn bowls essay for you, Sir.'

'Ah, yes!' Mudge looked so surprised he almost fell over. 'Bring it over.'

Davey threaded his way past chairs and desks and held out the essay to Mudge.

'Just put it on my desk,' Mudge said dismissively. 'I'll get to it later.'

'Yes, Sir.' Davey placed the essay on Mudge's desk.

Mudge peered at the title page and sniffed as if the essay somehow offended him.

'I imagine it won't take me long to read if it's your usual standard.'

Davey ignored Bella's look of triumph on the way back to his desk.

 118

The next few days passed in a blur for Davey. He worked with Trevor before and after school. He kept his head down in class and tried to be a model student. He helped Mudge polish endless supplies of lawn bowls during his lunch break. And when he could he practised his six-hitting.

All too soon, it was the night before the big game against Shimmer Bay.

Davey struggled to get to sleep. After a few hours of tossing and turning, he turned on his light and sat up in bed. Max gave a snort of protest but went back to sleep.

Davey looked up at the faded poster of his hero, Ricky Ponting, which hung above his bed. Ricky was smiling and, despite the fangs that Sunil had added, it gave Davey

confidence to imagine he was talking to the real Ricky.

Davey imagined Ricky was standing at the crease – he stared straight ahead, concentrating on the ball coming his way.

'Everyone's out to get me, Ricky,' Davey told his hero. 'I've set myself up for the impossible. And now all the people who want me to fail are going to get what they want.'

'It's not over until the last wicket falls.'

'What?' Davey could have sworn that Ricky had spoken, but the face in the poster just stared back at him.

Davey turned the phrase over and over in his mind and eventually fell asleep.

CHAPTER 13

AGAINST THE ODDS

Nothing could have prepared Davey for the size of the crowd gathered at the cricket ground.

'Holy moly,' he murmured.

Word of the bet had spread like wildfire throughout the school. Kids from kindy

through to Year Six were keen to see if Davey
Warner could indeed hit six sixes. Nobody
wanted to see him become Mo Clouter's
personal slave.

Davey noticed that most of 6M were there.
He could easily pick out Mo's big head. He
noticed that Bella was also in the crowd.

'You're going down, Shorty,' growled Mo
when he saw Davey. 'Prepare to lose.'

Davey gave Mo a friendly wave and scanned
the rest of the crowd.

Rob, the selector for the rep side, was there.
He was always on the lookout for new talent.
Seeing Rob made Davey's stomach lurch with
nerves.

'Davey Warner!' Rob nodded and waved his
little notebook.

Talk about pressure.

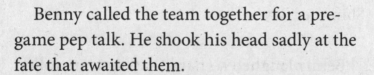

But the biggest surprise was that Benny
was there on time before the start of a
big game.

'So miracles do happen!' said Sunil. He and
Davey shared a look.

'Oi, Sluggers!'

Benny called the team together for a pre-
game pep talk. He shook his head sadly at the
fate that awaited them.

'It takes real courage to lose well,' Benny
began, and he adjusted his belt over his
protruding belly. 'The fact that you guys have
got this far should be reward enough.'

For once, Benny was right. There was a
general muttering of agreement from the

team. After all, everyone knew that Shimmer Bay were virtually impossible to beat.

'I even heard a joke that Davey is going to hit six sixes!' Benny grabbed his generous stomach and let out a huge belly laugh. 'Funniest thing I've ever heard, hey Warner?'

Davey cleared his throat. 'It's true, Coach. What's more, we're going to win. We're going to beat Josh Jarrett and Shimmer Bay.'

Benny laughed so hard that big tears rolled down his chubby cheeks. 'You boys, you keep me young.' He wiped the tears away. 'I need to go and eat something before the game.' He belched loudly and wandered off towards the canteen.

Sunil gathered the team in closer.

'Davey's right,' said Sunil in his captain's voice.

It was hard not to get carried away by Sunil's sunny disposition and sense of authority. 'We've got this far because we're good. We're going to take this team down and claim our rightful spot at number one!'

The team let out a cheer.

The Sluggers won the toss and opted to bat first. Because it was such a big game, it was going to be played over two innings. They had their work cut out for them.

As Shimmer Bay made their way out onto the field, Josh Jarrett tipped his cap curtly to Davey.

'Hey Warner, I see your bowling cronies are here to support you!' He held up his

thumb and forefinger in the shape of an
L for 'loser'.

Davey didn't know what Josh was talking
about until he saw a small group gathered
under a tree. Trevor and a few of the other
guys from the bowls club were sipping tea
from plastic mugs.

'Bowl me over!' Davey chuckled to himself.
Just about everyone he knew was gathered
together to watch this game.

Then Davey saw something that nearly did
bowl him over.

Mudge was standing with Trevor.

It made *no* sense. Mudge hated cricket!
He *detested* cricket. Davey didn't have time
to figure out Mudge's agenda, because it was
time to play.

The Sluggers got off to a shaky start, losing their two openers early in quick succession.

It was Davey's turn to bat. This was his big moment.

As he walked out, Sunil gave him a big thumbs up.

'Go, Davey!' called his family.

Despite the crowd watching his every move, Davey did his best to block everything out. It was him and Kaboom and the ball. He tightened his grip and tapped Kaboom against the crease.

'Let's see what you've got, Warner,' snarled Troy, Shimmer Bay's fast bowler.

Davey felt quietly confident and started hitting the ball very sweetly. He kept his head down and allowed himself to warm up.

Before too long, he had reached thirty-five, with two well-struck sixes under his belt.

'Boo!' Mo jeered.

'You can do it, Davey!' Trevor yelled. The bowlers let out a whoop.

Davey grinned and then, in a rush of over-confidence, he decided to try the helicopter shot.

He hit the ball high on the bat and succeeded only in looping it to backward square leg, where the fielder took an easy catch.

He was out.

George got his head down and, with some help from Tay Tui, they pushed the score on to 128 all out.

When Shimmer Bay came in, they started
steadily, with Josh batting well. However, Sunil
was at his deadly best. He dismissed three of
their top order and continued to trouble all
the batsmen.

When Josh was on forty-two and the
Shimmers were three down for eighty, Sunil
enticed Josh to play at one outside the off
stump. It left him just enough to catch the
edge of his bat and wicket-keeper Tay took
a straightforward catch.

The remaining Shimmer batsmen managed
a few more runs, but eventually they were all
out for 116, with Sunil taking seven wickets.

In the Sluggers' second innings, they
again lost their opening batsmen early.
Davey was well aware of the responsibility
he carried and played within himself
while he accumulated runs.

With the score on two wickets for sixty-two, the Shimmers' fast bowler tried a short of a length delivery at Davey. He stepped inside the line and smacked it straight over the square leg fence.

Clearly annoyed, Troy bowled another, even faster, ball but Davey repeated the dose.

He had now hit four sixes.

'Way to go, Davey!' his dad shouted.

'Two to go,' Davey said to himself.

The Sluggers lost another wicket, but Davey bided his time, waiting for the right ball. At three for ninety-four, with Davey now on forty-six, their off-spinner tossed one up. Davey took two paces down the pitch and hit it straight over his head and over the sightscreen. Five sixes!

The crowd erupted as, with the shot, he brought up the team's hundred and his own half-century. Davey clocked Mo looking worried.

Davey realised that his arms and shoulders had held up. He wasn't as tired as he thought he would be.

Trevor . . . ! Davey thought. He realised that all the work he'd done at the bowling club had given him the upper body strength he needed.

Several overs later, the Sluggers had a good lead and Davey was in the sixties.

It's now or never, Davey thought, with the last over about to be bowled.

Davey tried the helicopter shot on a well-pitched ball from their medium-pacer. He swung himself almost off his feet and the

ball left the bat like a bullet from a gun. Davey heard the crowd gasp as the ball soared over wide mid-on.

He'd done it! Six sixes!

The crowd went ballistic. Davey Warner had hit six sixes and won the bet.

Sunil ran to Davey from the non-striker's end and nearly knocked him over with a hug.

'That was incredible!'

Davey felt completely stunned.

'Where's Clouter?' Davey asked Sunil. 'I feel like a Whopper Chomp or twenty.'

The friends scanned the crowd to see Mo taking off from the grounds as fast as his legs could carry him.

CHAPTER 14

THUGS, SLUGS AND BEAR HUGS

At the break between innings, Davey found himself surrounded by friends and well-wishers. People were lining up to congratulate him.

'Knew you could do it, kid brother.' Steve ruffled Davey's hair.

Trevor shook Davey's hand enthusiastically.

'Good for you!' Benny enveloped Davey in a bear hug. 'I was backing you all the way, son.'

'Warner?'

A familiar voice caused Davey to turn. 'Sir?'

Mudge looked so grim that Davey knew for sure he was a goner. It made sense now. Mudge couldn't wait until school to tell him he'd failed his assignment.

'I read your essay on preparing the green in order to play a game of lawn bowls.'

Davey noticed Bella Ferosi sidling up next to them. *Her ears must be flapping*, he thought. He'd be decked out in pink in no time.

'Yes, Sir?'

Mudge suddenly broke into a smile.

'I am pleased to say that you surprised me, Warner. The depth of research that you went into was impressive. And I have to say it gave me a new appreciation for the game of cricket.'

Davey's jaw dropped.

'I have given you an A.'

Bella scowled.

Davey's jaw dropped even further.

'What's more, I've sent your name to Mrs Trundle for the next round of merit awards. I think you'd better be on time to assembly on Monday.'

'Thank you, Sir,' Davey managed to say.

Was Davey's hearing working? Did Mudge just give him an A for his essay *and* a merit award?

He must have, because Bella was now trying to sneak away.

'Not so fast, Ferosi, you're not going anywhere!' He grabbed Bella's arm. 'We have a beautiful slug costume with your name on it.'

Bella shot Davey a withering look, but she went with Sunil and George.

Davey wolfed down an orange and then it was time to head out to field. After all, they still had a game to win.

The Sluggers weren't out of the woods.

Thanks to Davey's innings, they were leading by 147 runs, but the Shimmers were still very much in the game.

Josh was in great form. He'd taken Davey hitting six sixes badly and wasn't about to let go of the game. He smashed another four to the fence.

Despite excellent bowling from Sunil, the Shimmers were scoring quickly. The Sluggers' morale was dropping steadily and Sunil gathered the team together for a quick pep talk.

'We can do this!' he said cheerily in his captain's voice. 'After all, we have a secret weapon!'

'First I've heard of it!' Ivy said drily.

'What's our secret weapon?' asked Tay.

'That!' Sunil pointed to an odd-looking slug-coloured creature standing on the sidelines. Two limp antennae drooped from the top of its head.

The Sluggers' slug mascot had arrived.

'What *is* that thing?' cried Josh in horror.

'The slug!' cried the team.

A huge cheer rang out from the Sluggers supporters. Despite burning cheeks and looking as if she might die of embarrassment, Bella Ferosi began to perform the slug dance. To her credit, she gave it all she had.

'Sluggers! Sluggers!' chanted the crowd.

Though wickets fell at regular intervals, Josh continued to play very well. He was like a man possessed. He handled all the Sluggers bowlers, including Sunil, with ease.

With the score at seven wickets down for 144 and Josh at the crease, things were looking grim for the Sluggers.

Sunil brought himself back on for one last effort.

Josh edged the first ball on the ground through the slips cordon and ran a single: seven for 145.

Next ball, with a mighty effort, Sunil produced an unplayable delivery that pitched on leg stump and seamed away to knock the batsman's off stump out of the ground: eight for 145.

The Shimmers' number ten came in looking distinctly nervous. Sunil bounded in and pitched a full one straight at his toes. He backed away but managed to get his bat up, and the ball looped in the air to point, where Davey took a simple catch.

The score was now nine for 145.

In came the Shimmers' number eleven. Sunil was again in top form. He got the batsman to edge the ball, but even Tay, flinging herself to her right, could not hold the difficult chance.

Josh rushed through for a single to get the strike.

Sunil bowled to Josh as fast as he possibly could, but over-pitched.

Josh slammed the full toss back down the wicket straight at Sunil. He valiantly tried to catch it, but it burst through his hands and hit him on the inside of the kneecap.

'Oohhh!' gasped the crowd.

Sunil went down like a sack of spuds, writhing in pain.

No run was taken and the Sluggers crowded around their captain. He definitely couldn't bowl any more and was helped off the field.

Shimmer Bay needed only two runs to win.

One wicket to fall.

One ball left in the over.

Who was going to bowl it?

'Give it to me,' said Davey. 'I'll bowl.'

He and Josh Jarrett locked eyes.

CHAPTER 15

'IT'S NOT OVER UNTIL THE LAST WICKET FALLS'

Davey had noticed when he was batting that at the crease where Josh stood there were one or two cracks in the pitch outside the off stump.

If he could land the ball on one, he might just get it to move around a bit.

'Ha!' Josh smirked as Davey got ready to bowl. 'The lawn bowler! Perfect.'

Josh had no idea just how right he was. Davey was a lawn bowler and a greenkeeper. But he was also a cricketer.

'This one's for Josh,' Davey told the ball.

Davey ran in holding the ball with his fingers on either side of the seam. The ball pitched a little short and Josh stepped back, intending to smack it away on the off side.

But the ball caught the edge of the crack and seamed wickedly back in to Josh. Completely surprised, Josh only succeeded in getting a thin inside edge.

Tay flung herself to her left at full stretch and just managed to glove the ball in her left hand.

Josh Jarrett was out! Tay and Davey had done it between them.

The Sluggers had won by one run.

'YAAAYYY!'

The new number ones on the ladder sprinted around the pitch faster than any slug you've ever seen. Even the slug got into the spirit. Bella was picked up by the crowd and carried around the field. The Sluggers were heroes!

It had been a sensational weekend, but Monday came around as quickly as ever.

As Davey pulled up at the school gate, he noticed Mo and his mates lurking.

'Wondered when you'd show up!'
Davey held out his hand for the suitcase.
'Hand it over.'

Then Davey noticed Mo's face.

'You look awful,' Davey said. He wasn't
trying to be mean. Mo *did* look awful. He
looked green and shiny. He was sweating
profusely and his hair hung limply on his
head. In fact, he looked more like a slug than
Bella had in costume.

'I'm sick,' Mo groaned. 'Something I ate . . .'

Mo looked like he might projectile-vomit
any second. Davey took a step back.

'Anyway, my dad said all Clouters hold up
their end of the bet, so . . .' Mo handed over to
Davey the Whopper Chomps suitcase.

'Thanks, Mo. It takes a big man to admit when he's wrong.'

Mo began to back away slowly.

Davey unzipped the suitcase to reveal . . . nothing. The case was empty.

'Hey!' Davey called to Mo's retreating back.

'Sucker!' Mo turned and jeered. 'Then he clutched his stomach. 'I think I'm going to throw up . . .' He headed for the toilets at a rapid pace. 'Too many Whopper Chomps . . .'

He couldn't have eaten all twenty packets on his own, could he?

The bell rang.

For once, Davey Warner was on time for assembly.

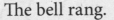

Mrs Trundle made a few announcements and then began to read through a list of names of recent merit award winners. She paused before the fourth name.

'Just a minute,' she said, before a hushed conversation with Mudge.

'No mistake, Lavinia, I mean, Mrs Trundle,' Mudge crooned, rocking back and forth on his heels.

Both of Trundle's eyes twitched madly. 'David Warner,' she called, with a slight catch in her voice.

Davey stood up and wound his way past students to the front of assembly.

'Thank you.' Davey took his piece of paper and nodded to the cheering throng of kids in front of him. He scanned the faces he knew so well.

He felt pretty good. The Sandhill Sluggers were number one on the ladder. He'd hit six sixes in a game. He'd got Josh Jarrett out. Bella Ferosi had dressed as a slug. His folks were happy with him for getting an A. He'd beaten Mo in a bet. He had won his first-ever merit award.

Most importantly, it was only one week until the holidays. Davey and his mates were going to play endless games of cricket.

And NOTHING was going to get in their way.

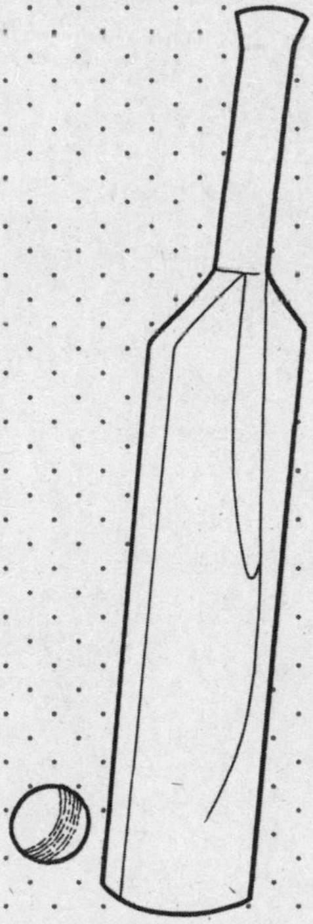

DAVID WARNER'S AMAZING STATS

DAVID ANDREW WARNER

BORN: 27 OCTOBER 1986

BATS: LEFT HANDED

BOWLS: RIGHT ARM LEG BREAK

	Test (2011-)*	ODI (2009-)*	T20 (2009-)*
Matches:	35	50	52
Total runs:	3028	1539	1444
Highest score:	180	163	90
Batting average:	48.06	31.41	29.47
Scoring rate:	74.14	83.51	138.85
Centuries:	11	2	-
Sixes:	30	23	66

*CURRENT AT 5 JANUARY 2015

YOUR AMAZING CRICKET STATS

NAME: ....

BORN: ....

BATS: ....

BOWLS: ....

HIGHEST SCORE: ....

MOST SIXES: ....

MOST CATCHES IN ONE MATCH: ....

MOST EMBARRASSING MOMENT: ....

....

....

TOUGHEST OPPOSITION: ....

FAVOURITE AUSTRALIAN PLAYER: ....

FAVOURITE INTERNATIONAL PLAYER:

....

ULTIMATE DREAM TEAM: ....

....

....

....

....

....

....